Woodrow Wilson

Why We Are at War; Messages to the Congress January to April 1917

in large print

 MEGALI

Woodrow Wilson

Why We Are at War; Messages to the Congress January to April 1917

in large print

Reproduction of the original.

1st Edition 2023 | ISBN: 978-3-38705-898-7

Megali Verlag is an imprint of Outlook Verlagsgesellschaft mbH.

Verlag (Publisher): Outlook Verlag GmbH, Zeilweg 44, 60439 Frankfurt, Deutschland
Vertretungsberechtigt (Authorized to represent): E. Roepke, Zeilweg 44, 60439 Frankfurt, Deutschland
Druck (Print): Books on Demand GmbH, In de Tarpen 42, 22848 Norderstedt, Deutschland

WHY WE ARE AT WAR

Messages to the Congress
January to April 1917

BY

WOODROW WILSON

Messages to the Congress January to April, 1917 by Woodrow Wilson, President of the United States, with the President's proclamation of war April 6, 1917 and his message to the American people April 15, 1917.

PUBLISHER'S NOTE

This book presents in convenient form the memorable messages to the Congress read by President Wilson in January, February, and April, 1917. They should be read together, for only in this way is it possible to appreciate both the forbearance and the logic of events reflected in these consecutive chapters of history. While the great war message of April 2d is obviously the most momentous, its full significance is not made clear unless it is read as the climax of the preceding messages and also in connection with the President's proclamation of a state of war on April 6th and his message to the American people of April 15th. While the approval of President Wilson was very naturally requested and obtained for the publication of these messages in collected form, the Publishers are responsible for the title and for captions. They have felt that they are rendering a service of permanent value by collecting and presenting these historic documents in the same form in which they have published President Wilson's *When a Man Comes to Himself, On Being Human,* and *The President of the United States.*

I.
A WORLD LEAGUE FOR PEACE

Message to the Senate
January 22, 1917

Gentlemen of the Senate:

On the 18th of December last I addressed an identic note to the Governments of the nations now at war, requesting them to state, more definitely than they had yet been stated by either group of belligerents, the terms upon which they would deem it possible to make peace. I spoke on behalf of humanity and of the rights of all neutral nations like our own, many of whose most vital interests the war puts in constant jeopardy.

The Central Powers united in a reply which stated merely that they were ready to meet their antagonists in conference to discuss terms of peace.

ENTENTE REPLY WAS MORE DEFINITE

The Entente Powers have replied much more definitely and have stated, in general terms, indeed, but with sufficient definiteness to imply details, the arrangements, guarantees, and acts of reparation which they deem to be the indispensable conditions of a satisfactory settlement.

We are that much nearer a definite discussion of the peace which shall end the present war. We are that much nearer the discussion of the international concert which must thereafter hold the world at peace.

In every discussion of the peace that must end this war it is taken for granted that that peace must be followed by some definite concert of power which will make it virtually impossible that any such catastrophe should ever overwhelm us again. Every lover of mankind, every sane and thoughtful man, must take that for granted.

I have sought this opportunity to address you because I thought that I owed it to you, as the council associated with me in the final determination of our international obligations, to disclose to you, without reserve, the thought and purpose that have been taking form in my mind in regard to the duty of our Government in these days to come when it will be necessary to lay afresh and upon a new plan the foundations of peace among the nations.

DECLARES PEACE IS NOT FAR OFF

It is inconceivable that the people of the United States should play no part in that great enterprise. To take part in such a service will be the opportunity for which they have sought to prepare themselves by the very principles and purposes of their polity and the approved practices of their Government, ever since the days when they set up a new nation in the high and honorable hope that it might in all that it was and did show mankind the way to liberty.

They cannot, in honor, withhold the service to which they are now about to be challenged. They do not wish to withhold it. But they owe it to themselves and to the other nations of the world to state the conditions under which they will feel free to render it. That service is nothing less than this—to add their authority and their power to the authority and force of other nations to guarantee peace and justice throughout the world. Such a settlement cannot now be long postponed. It is right that before it comes this Government should frankly formulate the conditions upon which it would feel justified in asking our people to approve its formal and solemn adherence to a league for peace. I am here to attempt to state those conditions.

MUST NOT SERVE SELFISH AIMS

The present war must first be ended; but we owe it to candor and to a just regard for the opinion of mankind to say that so far as our participation in guarantees of future peace is concerned it makes a great deal of difference in what way and upon what terms it is ended. The treaties and agreements which bring it to an end must embody terms which will create a peace that is worth guaranteeing and preserving, a peace that will win the approval of mankind;

not merely a peace that will serve the several interests and immediate aims of the nations engaged.

We shall have no voice in determining what those terms shall be, but we shall, I feel sure, have a voice in determining whether they shall be made lasting or not by the guarantees of a universal covenant, and our judgment upon what is fundamental and essential as a condition precedent to permanency should be spoken now, not afterward, when it may be too late.

No covenant of co-operative peace that does not include the peoples of the New World can suffice to keep the future safe against war, and yet there is only one sort of peace that the peoples of America could join in guaranteeing.

The elements of that peace must be elements that engage the confidence and satisfy the principles of the American Governments, elements consistent with their political faith and the practical convictions which the peoples of America have once for all embraced and undertaken to defend.

WORLD ALLIANCE IS NECESSARY

I do not mean to say that any American Government would throw any obstacle in the way of any terms of peace the Governments now at war might agree upon, or seek to upset them when made, whatever they might be. I only take it for granted that mere terms of peace between the belligerents will not satisfy even the belligerents themselves.

Mere agreements may not make peace secure. It will be absolutely necessary that a force be created as a guarantor of the permanency of the settlement so much greater than the force of any nation now engaged in any alliance hitherto formed or projected that no nation, no probable combination of nations, could face or withstand it.

If the peace presently to be made is to endure it must be a peace made secure by the organized major force of mankind.

The terms of the immediate peace agreed upon will determine whether it is a peace for which such a guarantee can be secured. The question upon which the whole future peace and policy of the world depends is this:

Is the present war a struggle for a just and secure peace or only for a new balance of power? If it be only a struggle for a new balance of power, who will guarantee, who can guarantee, the stable equilibrium of the new arrangement?

NO VICTORY FOR EITHER SIDE

Only a tranquil Europe can be a stable Europe. There must be not only a balance of power, but a community of power; not organized rivalries, but an organized common peace.

Fortunately, we have received very explicit assurances on this point. The statesmen of both of the groups of nations now arrayed against one another have said, in terms that could not be misinterpreted, that it was no part of the purpose they had in mind to crush their antagonists. But the implications of these assurances may not be equally clear to all—may not be the same on both sides of the water. I think it will be serviceable if I attempt to set forth what we understand them to be.

They imply, first of all, that it must be a peace without victory. It is not pleasant to say this. I beg that I may be permitted to put my own interpretation upon it and that it may be understood that no other interpretation was in my thought.

I am seeking only to face realities and to face them without soft concealments. Victory would mean peace forced upon the loser, a victor's terms imposed upon the vanquished. It would be accepted in humiliation, under duress, at an intolerable sacrifice, and would leave a sting, a resentment, a bitter memory, upon which terms of peace would rest, not permanently, but only as upon quicksand.

Only a peace between equals can last; only a peace the very principle of which is equality and a common participation in a common benefit. The right state of mind, the right feeling between nations, is as necessary for a lasting peace as is the just settlement of questions of territory or of racial and national allegiance.

MUST EQUALIZE RIGHTS OF NATIONS

The equality of nations upon which peace must be founded, if it is to last, must be an equality of rights; the guarantees exchanged must neither recognize nor imply a difference between big nations and small, between those that are powerful and those that are weak.

Right must be based upon the common strength, not upon the individual strength, of the nations upon whose concert peace will depend.

Equality of territory or of resources there, of course, cannot be; nor any other sort of equality not gained in the ordinary peaceful and legitimate development of the peoples themselves. But no one asks or expects anything more than an equality of rights. Mankind is looking now for freedom of life, not for equipoises of power.

And there is a deeper thing involved than even equality of rights among organized nations. No peace can last, or ought to last, which does not recognize and accept the principle that Governments derive all their just powers from the consent of the governed, and that no right anywhere exists to hand people about from sovereignty to sovereignty as if they were property.

I take it for granted, for instance, if I may venture upon a single example, that statesmen everywhere are agreed that there should be a united, independent, and autonomous Poland, and that henceforth inviolable security of life, of worship, and of industrial and social development should be guaranteed to all peoples who have lived hitherto under the power of Governments devoted to a faith and purpose hostile to their own.

I speak of this, not because of any desire to exalt an abstract political principle which has always been held very dear by those who have sought to build up liberty in America, but for the same reason that I have spoken of the other conditions of peace which seem to me clearly indispensable—because I wish frankly to uncover realities.

CRUSHED PEOPLES WILL REVOLT

Any peace which does not recognize and accept this principle will inevitably be upset. It will not rest upon the affections or the convictions of mankind. The ferment of spirit of whole populations will fight subtly and constantly against it, and all the world will sympathize. The world can be at peace only if its life is stable, and there can be no stability where the will is in rebellion, where there is not tranquillity of spirit and a sense of justice, of freedom, and of right.

So far as practicable, moreover, every great people now struggling toward a full development of its resources and of its powers should be assured a direct outlet to the great highways of the sea. Where this cannot be done by the cession of territory, it can no doubt be done by the neutralization of direct rights of way under the general guarantee which will assure the peace itself. With a right comity of arrangement no nation need be shut away from free access to the open paths of the world's commerce.

And the paths of the sea must alike in law and in fact be free. The freedom of the seas is the *sine qua non* of peace, equality, and co-operation.

No doubt a somewhat radical reconsideration of many of the rules of international practice hitherto sought to be established may be necessary in order to make the seas indeed free and common in practically all circumstances for the use of mankind, but the motive for such changes is convincing and compelling. There can be no trust or intimacy between the peoples of the world without them.

The free, constant, unthreatened intercourse of nations is an essential part of the process of peace and of development. It need not be difficult to define or to secure the freedom of the seas if the Governments of the world sincerely desire to come to an agreement concerning it.

REQUIRES LIMITATION OF ARMAMENTS

It is a problem closely connected with the limitation of naval armaments and the co-operation of the navies of the world in keeping the seas at once free and safe. And the question of limiting naval armaments opens the wider and perhaps more difficult question of the limitation of armies and of all programs of military preparation.

Difficult and delicate as these questions are, they must be faced with the utmost candor and decided in a spirit of real accommodation if peace is to come with healing in its wings and come to stay. Peace cannot be had without concession and sacrifice. There can be no sense of safety and equality among the nations if great preponderating armies are henceforth to continue here and there to be built up and maintained.

The statesmen of the world must plan for peace, and nations must adjust and accommodate their policy to it as they have planned for war and made ready for pitiless contest and rivalry. The question of armaments, whether on land or sea, is the most immediately and intensely practical question connected with the future fortunes of nations and of mankind.

I have spoken upon these great matters without reserve and with the utmost explicitness because it has seemed to me to be necessary if the world's yearning desire for peace was anywhere to find free voice and utterance. Perhaps I am the only person in high authority among all the peoples of the world who is at liberty to speak and hold nothing back.

I am speaking as an individual, and yet I am speaking also, of course, as the responsible head of a great Government, and I feel confident that I have said what the people of the United States would wish me to say. May I not add that I hope and believe that I am in effect speaking for liberals and friends of humanity in every nation and of every program of liberty?

I would fain believe that I am speaking for the silent mass of mankind everywhere who have as yet had no place or opportunity to speak their real hearts out concerning the death and ruin they see to have come already upon the persons and the homes they hold most dear.

SEES WORLD-WIDE MONROE DOCTRINE

And in holding out the expectation that the people and Government of the United States will join the other civilized nations of the world in guaranteeing the permanence of peace upon such terms as I have named, I speak with the greater boldness and confidence because it is clear to every man who can think that there is in this promise no breach in either our traditions or our policy as a nation, but a fulfilment, rather, of all that we have professed or striven for.

I am proposing, as it were, that the nations should with one accord adopt the doctrine of President Monroe as the doctrine of the world; that no nation should seek to extend its polity over any other nation or people, but that every people should be left free to determine its own polity, its own way of development, unhindered, unthreatened, unafraid, the little along with the great and powerful.

I am proposing that all nations henceforth avoid entangling alliances which would draw them into competitions of power, catch them in a net of intrigue and selfish rivalry, and disturb their own affairs with influences intruded from without. There is no entangling alliance in a concert of power. When all unite to act in the same sense and with the same purpose, all act in the common interest and are free to live their own lives under a common protection.

I am proposing government by the consent of the governed; that freedom of the seas which in international conference after conference representatives of the United States have urged with the eloquence of those who are the convinced disciples of liberty; and that moderation of armaments which makes of armies and navies a power for order merely, not an instrument of aggression or of selfish violence.

These are American principles, American policies. We can stand for no others. And they are also the principles and policies of forward-looking men and women everywhere, of every modern nation, of every enlightened community. They are the principles of mankind, and must prevail.

II.
THE SEVERANCE OF DIPLOMATIC RELATIONS WITH GERMANY

Message to the Congress
February 3, 1917

Gentlemen of the Congress:

The Imperial German Government, on the 31st of January, announced to this Government and to the Governments of the other neutral nations that on and after the first day of February, the present month, it would adopt a policy with regard to the use of submarines against all shipping seeking to pass through certain designated areas of the high seas to which it is clearly my duty to call your attention.

Let me remind the Congress that on the 18th of April last, in view of the sinking on the 24th of March of the cross-Channel passenger-steamer *Sussex* by a German submarine, without summons or warning, and the consequent loss of the lives of several citizens of the United States who were passengers aboard her, this Government addressed a note to the Imperial German Government in which it made the following declaration:

If it is still the purpose of the Imperial German Government to prosecute relentless and indiscriminate warfare against vessels of commerce by the use of submarines without regard to what the Government of the United States must consider the sacred and indisputable rules of international law and the universally recognized dictates of humanity, the Government of the United States is at last forced to the conclusion that there is but one course it can pursue. Unless the German Government should now immediately declare and effect an abandonment of its present methods of submarine warfare against passenger and freight-carrying vessels the Government of the United States can have no choice but to sever diplomatic relations with the German Empire altogether.

GERMANY'S U-BOAT PLEDGE
In reply to this declaration the German Government gave this Government the following assurances:

The German Government is prepared to do its utmost to confine the operations of war for the rest of its duration to the fighting forces of the belligerents, thereby insuring the freedom of the seas, a principle upon which the German Government believes, now as before, to be in agreement with the Government of the United States.

The German Government, guided by this idea, notifies the Government of the United States that the German naval forces have received the following orders:

In accordance with the general principles of visit and search and destruction of merchant vessels recognized by international law, such vessels, both within and without the area declared as naval war zone, shall not be sunk without warning and without saving human lives, unless these ships attempt to escape or offer resistance.

But neutrals cannot expect that Germany, forced to fight for her existence, shall, for the sake of neutral interest, restrict the use of an effective weapon if her enemy is permitted to continue to apply at will methods of warfare violating the rules of international law. Such a demand would be incompatible with the character of neutrality, and the German Government is convinced that the Government of the United States does not think of making such a demand, knowing that the Government of the United States has repeatedly declared that it is determined to restore the principle of the freedom of the seas from whatever quarter it has been violated.

HOW THE UNITED STATES REPLIED

To this the Government of the United States replied on the 8th of May, accepting, of course, the assurances given, but adding:

The Government of the United States feels it necessary to state that it takes it for granted that the Imperial German Government does not intend to imply that the maintenance of its newly announced policy is in any way contingent upon the course or result of diplomatic negotiations between the

Government of the United States and any other belligerent Government, notwithstanding the fact that certain passages in the Imperial Government's note of the 4th instant might appear to be susceptible to that construction. In order, however, to avoid any possible misunderstanding, the Government of the United States notifies the Imperial Government that it cannot for a moment entertain, much less discuss, a suggestion that respect by German naval authorities for the rights of citizens of the United States upon the high seas should in any way or in the slightest degree be made contingent upon the conduct of any other Government affecting the rights of neutrals and non-combatants. Responsibility in such matters is single, not joint; absolute, not relative.

To this note of the 8th of May the Imperial German Government made no reply.

On the 31st of January, the Wednesday of the present week, the German Ambassador handed to the Secretary of State, along with a formal note, a memorandum which contains the following statement:

GERMANY'S NEW POLICY

The Imperial Government, therefore, does not doubt that the Government of the United States will understand the situation thus forced upon Germany by the Entente Allies' brutal methods of war and by their determination to destroy the Central Powers, and that the Government of the United States will further realize that the now openly disclosed intentions of the Entente Allies give back to Germany the freedom of action which she reserved in her note addressed to the Government of the United States on May 4, 1916.

Under these circumstances Germany will meet the illegal measures of her enemies by forcibly preventing, after February 1, 1917, in a zone around Great Britain, France, Italy, and in the eastern Mediterranean all navigation, that of neutrals included, from and to France, etc. All ships met within the zone will be sunk.

I think that you will agree with me that, in view of this declaration, which suddenly and without prior intimation of any kind deliberately withdraws the solemn assurance given in the Imperial Government's note of the 4th of May, 1916, this Government has no alternative consistent with the dignity and honor of the United States but to take the course which, in its note of the 18th of April, 1916, it announced that it would take in the event that the German Government did not declare and effect an abandonment of the methods of submarine warfare which it was then employing and to which it now purposes again to resort.

ALL RELATIONS BROKEN OFF

I have, therefore, directed the Secretary of State to announce to his Excellency the German ambassador that all diplomatic relations between the United States and the German Empire are severed, and that the American ambassador at Berlin will immediately be withdrawn, and, in accordance with this decision, to hand to his Excellency his passports.

Notwithstanding this unexpected action of the German Government, this sudden and deeply deplorable renunciation of its assurances, given this Government at one of the most critical moments of tension in the relations of the two Governments, I refuse to believe that it is the intention of the German authorities to do in fact what they have warned us they will feel at liberty to do. I cannot bring myself to believe that they will indeed pay no regard to the ancient friendship between their people and our own or to the solemn obligations which have been exchanged between them and destroy American ships and take the lives of American citizens in the wilful prosecution of the ruthless naval program they have announced their intention to adopt. Only actual overt acts on their part can make me believe it even now.

WILL PROTECT AMERICAN RIGHTS

If this inveterate confidence on my part in the sobriety and prudent foresight of their purpose should unhappily prove unfounded, if American ships and American lives should, in fact, be sacrificed by their naval commanders in heedless contravention of the just and reasonable understandings of international law and the obvious dictates of humanity, I shall take the liberty of coming again before the Congress to ask that authority be given me to use any means that may be necessary for the protection of our seamen and our people in the prosecution of their peaceful and legitimate errands on the high seas. I can do nothing less. I take it for granted that all neutral Governments will take the same course.

I do not desire any hostile conflict with the Imperial German Government. We are the sincere friends of the German people and earnestly desire to remain at peace with the Government which speaks for them. We shall not believe that they are hostile to us until we are obliged to believe it; and we purpose nothing more than the reasonable defense of the undoubted rights of our people. We wish to serve no selfish ends. We seek merely to stand true alike in thought and in action to the immemorial principles of our people which I sought to express in my address to the Senate only two weeks ago—seek merely to vindicate our right to liberty and justice and an unmolested life. These are bases of peace, not war. God grant we may not be challenged to defend them by acts of wilful injustice on the part of the Government of Germany.

III.
REQUEST FOR A GRANT OF POWER

Message to the Congress
February 26, 1917

Gentlemen of the Congress:

I have again asked the privilege of addressing you because we are moving through critical times, during which it seems to me to be my duty to keep in close touch with the Houses of Congress so that neither counsel nor action shall run at cross-purposes between us.

On the 3d of February I officially informed you of the sudden and unexpected action of the Imperial German Government in declaring its intention to disregard the promises it had made to this Government in April last and undertake immediate submarine operations against all commerce, whether of belligerents or of neutrals, that should seek to approach Great Britain and Ireland, the Atlantic coasts of Europe, or the harbors of the eastern Mediterranean, and to conduct those operations without regard to the established restrictions of international practice, without regard to any considerations of humanity, even, which might interfere with their object.

AMERICAN COMMERCE SUFFERS, BUT OTHER NEUTRALS FARE WORSE

That policy was forthwith put into practice. It has now been in active exhibition for nearly four weeks. Its practical results are not fully disclosed. The commerce of other neutral nations is suffering severely, but not, perhaps, very much more severely than it was already suffering before the 1st of February, when the new policy of the Imperial Government was put into operation.

We have asked the co-operation of the other neutral Governments to prevent these depredations, but I fear none of them has thought it wise to join us in any common course of action. Our own commerce has suffered, is suffering, rather in apprehension than in fact, rather because so many of our ships are timidly keeping to their home ports than because American ships have been sunk.

Two American vessels have been sunk, the *Housatonic* and the *Lyman M. Law*. The case of the *Housatonic*, which was carrying foodstuffs consigned to a London firm, was essentially like the case of the *Frye*, in which, it will be recalled, the German Government admitted its liability for damages, and the lives of the crew, as in the case of the *Frye*, were safeguarded with reasonable care.

THE RUTHLESS SINKING OF SCHOONER "LYMAN M. LAW"

The case of the *Law*, which was carrying lemon-box staves to Palermo, disclosed a ruthlessness of method which deserves grave condemnation, but was accompanied by no circumstances which might not have been expected at any time in connection with the use of the submarine against merchantmen as the German Government has used it.

In sum, therefore, the situation we find ourselves in with regard to the actual conduct of the German submarine warfare against commerce and its effects upon our own ships and people is substantially the same that it was when I addressed you on the 3d of February, except for the tying up of our shipping in our own ports because of the unwillingness of our ship-owners to risk their vessels at sea without insurance or adequate protection, and the very serious congestion of our commerce which has resulted, a congestion which is growing rapidly more and more serious every day.

This in itself might presently accomplish, in effect, what the new German submarine orders were meant to accomplish, so far as we are concerned. We can only say, therefore, that the overt act which I have ventured to hope the German commanders would in fact avoid has not occurred.

SPARED BY CIRCUMSTANCES NOT BY INSTRUCTIONS

But while this is happily true, it must be admitted that there have been certain additional indications and expressions of purpose on the part of the German press and the German authorities which have increased rather than lessened the impression that if our ships and our people are spared it will be because of fortunate circumstances or because the commanders of the German submarines which they may happen to encounter exercise an unexpected discretion and restraint, rather than because of the instructions under which those commanders are acting.

It would be foolish to deny that the situation is fraught with the gravest possibilities and dangers. No thoughtful man can fail to see that the necessity for definite action may come at any time, if we are in fact, and not in word merely, to defend our elementary rights as a neutral nation. It would be most imprudent to be unprepared.

I cannot in such circumstances be unmindful of the fact that the expiration of the term of the present Congress is immediately at hand by constitutional limitation, and that it would in all likelihood require an unusual length of time to assemble and organize the Congress which is to succeed it.

MAY NEED THE AUTHORITY TO ACT ANY MOMENT

I feel that I ought, in view of that fact, to obtain from you full and immediate assurance of the authority which I may need at any moment to exercise. No doubt I already possess that authority without special warrant of law by the plain implication of my constitutional duties and powers, but I prefer in the present circumstances not to act upon general implication. I wish to feel that the authority and the power of the Congress are behind me in whatever it may become necessary for me to do. We are jointly the servants of the people and must act together and in their spirit, so far as we can divine and interpret it.

No one doubts what it is our duty to do. We must defend our commerce and the lives of our people in the midst of the present trying circumstances with discretion, but with clear and steadfast purpose. Only the method and the extent remain to be chosen upon the occasion, if occasion should indeed arise.

Since it has unhappily proved impossible to safeguard our neutral rights by diplomatic means against the unwarranted infringements they are suffering at the hands of Germany, there may be no recourse but to armed neutrality, which we shall know how to maintain and for which there is abundant American precedent.

NOT CONTEMPLATING WAR, BUT WANTS TO BE READY

It is devoutly to be hoped that it will not be necessary to put armed forces anywhere into action. The American people do not desire it, and our desire is not different from theirs. I am sure that they will understand the spirit in which I am now acting, the purpose I hold nearest my heart, and would wish to exhibit in everything I do. I am anxious that the people of the nations at war also should understand and not mistrust us.

I hope that I need give no further proofs and assurances than I have already given throughout nearly three years of anxious patience that I am the friend of peace, and mean to preserve it for America so long as I am able.

I am not now proposing or contemplating war, or any steps that lead to it. I merely request that you will accord me by your own vote and definite bestowal the means and the authority to safeguard in practice the right of a great people, who are at peace and who are desirous of exercising none but the rights of peace, to follow the pursuit of peace in quietness and good-will—rights recognized time out of mind by all the civilized nations of the world.

No course of my choosing or of theirs will lead to war. War can come only by the wilful acts and aggressions of others.

ASKS POWER TO ARM SHIPS AND TO USE OTHER MEANS

You will understand why I can make no definite proposals or forecasts of action now, and must ask for your supporting authority in the most general terms. The form in which action may become necessary cannot yet be foreseen. I believe that the people will be willing to trust me to act with restraint, with prudence, and in the true spirit of amity and good faith that they have themselves displayed throughout these trying months; and it is in that belief that I request that you will authorize me to supply our merchant-ships with defensive arms should that become necessary, and with the means of using them, and to employ any other instrumentalities or methods that may be necessary and adequate to protect our ships and our people in their legitimate and peaceful pursuits of the seas.

I request also that you will grant me at the same time, along with the powers I ask, a sufficient credit to enable me to provide adequate means of protection where they are lacking, including adequate insurance against the present war risks.

I have spoken of our commerce and of the legitimate errands of our people on the seas, but you will not be misled as to my main thought, the thought that lies beneath these phrases and gives them dignity and weight.

CIVILIZATION AT STAKE IN ATTACK ON HUMAN RIGHTS

It is not of material interest merely that we are thinking. It is, rather, of fundamental human rights, chief of all the right of life itself. I am thinking not only of the rights of Americans to go and come about their proper business by way of the sea, but also of something much deeper, much more fundamental than that. I am thinking of those rights of humanity without which there is no civilization. My theme is of those great principles of compassion and of protection which mankind has sought to throw about human lives—the lives of non-combatants, the lives of men who are peacefully at work keeping the industrial processes of the world quick and vital, the lives of women and children, and of those who supply the labor which ministers to their sustenance.

We are speaking of no selfish material rights, but of rights which our hearts support, and whose foundation is that righteous passion for justice upon which all law, all structures alike of family, of state, and of mankind must rest, and upon the ultimate base of our existence and our liberty. I cannot imagine any man with American principles at his heart hesitating to defend these things.

IV.
WE MUST ACCEPT WAR

Message to the Congress
April 2, 1917

Gentlemen of the Congress:

I have called the Congress into extraordinary session because there are serious, very serious, choices of policy to be made, and made immediately, which it was neither right nor constitutionally permissible that I should assume the responsibility of making.

On the 3d of February last I officially laid before you the extraordinary announcement of the Imperial German Government that on and after the first day of February it was its purpose to put aside all restraints of law or of humanity and use its submarines to sink every vessel that sought to approach either the ports of Great Britain and Ireland or the western coasts of Europe or any of the ports controlled by the enemies of Germany within the Mediterranean. That had seemed to be the object of the German submarine warfare earlier in the war, but since April of last year the Imperial Government had somewhat restrained the commanders of its undersea craft in conformity with its promise then given to us that passenger-boats should not be sunk, and that due warning would be given to all other vessels which its submarines might seek to destroy when no resistance was offered or escape attempted, and care taken that their crews were given at least a fair chance to save their lives in their open boats.

The precautions taken were meager and haphazard enough, as was proved in distressing instance after instance in the progress of the cruel and unmanly business, but a certain degree of restraint was observed.

GERMANY'S RUTHLESS POLICY

The new policy has swept every restriction aside. Vessels of every kind, whatever their flag, their character, their cargo, their destination, their errand, have been ruthlessly sent to the bottom without warning, and without thought of help or mercy for those on board, the vessels of friendly neutrals along with those of belligerents. Even hospital-ships and ships carrying relief to the sorely bereaved and stricken people of Belgium, though the latter were provided with safe conduct through the proscribed areas by the German Government itself and were distinguished by unmistakable marks of identity, have been sunk with the same reckless lack of compassion or of principle.

I was for a little while unable to believe that such things would, in fact, be done by any Government that had hitherto subscribed to the humane practices of civilized nations. International law had its origin in the attempt to set up some law which would be respected and observed upon the seas, where no nation had right of dominion, and where lay the free highways of the world. By painful stage after stage has that law been built up with meager enough results, indeed, after all was accomplished that could be accomplished, but always with a clear view at least of what the heart and conscience of mankind demanded.

This minimum of right the German Government has swept aside under the plea of retaliation and necessity, and because it had no weapons which it could use at sea except these, which it is impossible to employ as it is employing them without throwing to the winds all scruples of humanity or of respect for the understandings that were supposed to underlie the intercourse of the world.

I am not now thinking of the loss of property involved, immense and serious as that is, but only of the wanton and wholesale destruction of the lives of non-combatants, men, women, and children engaged in pursuits which have always, even in the darkest periods of modern history, been deemed innocent and legitimate. Property can be paid for; the lives of peaceful and innocent people cannot be.

GERMAN WARFARE AGAINST MANKIND

The present German warfare against commerce is a warfare against mankind. It is a war against all nations. American ships have been sunk, American lives taken, in ways which it has stirred us very deeply to learn of, but the ships and people of other neutral and friendly nations have been sunk and overwhelmed in the waters in the same way. There has been no discrimination. The challenge is to all mankind. Each nation must decide for itself how it will meet it. The choice we make for ourselves must be made with a moderation of counsel and a temperateness of judgment befitting our character and our motives as a nation. We must put excited feeling away.

Our motive will not be revenge or the victorious assertion of the physical might of the nation, but only the vindication of right, of human right, of which we are only a single champion.

When I addressed the Congress on the 26th of February last I thought that it would suffice to assert our neutral rights with arms, our right to use the seas against unlawful interference, our right to keep our people safe against unlawful violence. But armed neutrality, it now appears, is impracticable. Because submarines are in effect outlaws when used as the German submarines have been used against merchant shipping, it is impossible to defend ships against their attacks as the law of nations has assumed that merchantmen would defend themselves against privateers or cruisers, visible craft giving chase upon the open sea.

It is common prudence in such circumstances, grim necessity, indeed, to endeavor to destroy them before they have shown their own intention. They must be dealt with upon sight, if dealt with at all.

The German Government denies the right of neutrals to use arms at all within the areas of the sea which it has proscribed, even in the defense of rights which no modern publicist has ever before questioned their right to defend. The intimation is conveyed that the armed guards which we have placed on our merchant-ships will be treated as beyond the pale of law and subject to be dealt with as pirates would be.

Armed neutrality is ineffectual enough at best; in such circumstances and in the face of such pretensions it is worse than ineffectual; it is likely to produce what it was meant to prevent; it is practically certain to draw us into the war without either the rights or the effectiveness of belligerents. There is one choice we cannot make, we are incapable of making: we will not choose the path of submission and suffer the most sacred rights of our nation and our people to be ignored or violated. The wrongs against which we now array ourselves are not common wrongs; they reach out to the very roots of human life.

BELLIGERENCY THRUST UPON US

With a profound sense of the solemn and even tragical character of the step I am taking and of the grave responsibilities which it involves, but in unhesitating obedience to what I deem my constitutional duty, I advise that the Congress declare the recent course of the Imperial German Government to be in fact nothing less than war against the Government and people of the United States. That it formally accept the status of belligerent which has thus been thrust upon it and that it take immediate steps not only to put the country in a more thorough state of defense, but also to exert all its power and employ all its resources to bring the Government of the German Empire to terms and end the war.

WHAT THIS WILL INVOLVE

What this will involve is clear. It will involve the utmost practicable co-operation in counsel and action with the Governments now at war with Germany, and as incident to that the extension to those Governments of the most liberal financial credits in order that our resources may so far as possible be added to theirs.

It will involve the organization and mobilization of all the material resources of the country to supply the materials of war and serve the incidental needs of the nation in the most abundant and yet the most economical and efficient way possible.

It will involve the immediate full equipment of the navy in all respects, but particularly in supplying it with the best means of dealing with the enemy's submarines.

It will involve the immediate addition to the armed forces of the United States already provided for by law in case of war at least 500,000 men, who should, in my opinion, be chosen upon the principle of universal liability to service, and also the authorization of subsequent additional increments of equal force so soon as they may be needed and can be handled in training.

It will involve also, of course, the granting of adequate credits to the Government, sustained, I hope, so far as they can equitably be sustained by the present generation, by well-conceived taxation. I say sustained so far as may be equitable by taxation because it seems to me that it would be most unwise to base the credits which will now be necessary entirely on money borrowed.

It is our duty, I most respectfully urge, to protect our people so far as we may against the very serious hardships and evils which would be likely to arise out of the inflation which would be produced by vast loans.

In carrying out the measures by which these things are to be accomplished we should keep constantly in mind the wisdom of interfering as little as possible in our own preparation and in the equipment of our own military forces with the duty—for it will be a very practical duty—of supplying the nations already at war with Germany with the materials which they can obtain only from us or by our assistance. They are in the field and we should help them in every way to be effective there.

I shall take the liberty of suggesting, through the several executive departments of the Government, for the consideration of your committees measures for the accomplishment of the several objects I have mentioned. I hope that it will be your pleasure to deal with them as having been framed after very careful thought by the branch of the Government upon which the responsibility of conducting the war and safeguarding the nation will most directly fall.

OUR MOTIVES AND OBJECTS

While we do these things, these deeply momentous things, let us be very clear and make very clear to all the world what our motives and our objects are. My own thought has not been driven from its habitual and normal course by the unhappy events of the last two months, and I do not believe that the thought of the nation has been altered or clouded by them.

I have exactly the same thing in mind now that I had in mind when I addressed the Senate on the 22d of January last; the same that I had in mind when I addressed the Congress on the 3d of February and on the 26th of February.

Our object now, as then, is to vindicate the principles of peace and justice in the life of the world as against selfish and autocratic power and to set up amongst the really free and self-governed peoples of the world such a concert of purpose and of action as will henceforth insure the observance of those principles.

Neutrality is no longer feasible or desirable where the peace of the world is involved and the freedom of its peoples, and the menace to that peace and freedom lies in the existence of autocratic Governments backed by organized force which is controlled wholly by their will, not by the will of their people. We have seen the last of neutrality in such circumstances.

We are at the beginning of an age in which it will be insisted that the same standards of conduct and of responsibility for wrong done shall be observed among nations and their Governments that are observed among the individual citizens of civilized states.

We have no quarrel with the German people. We have no feeling toward them but one of sympathy and friendship. It was not upon their impulse that their Government acted in entering this war. It was not with their previous knowledge or approval.

It was a war determined upon as wars used to be determined upon in the old, unhappy days when peoples were nowhere consulted by their rulers and wars were provoked and waged in the interest of dynasties or of little groups of ambitious men who were accustomed to use their fellow-men as pawns and tools.

Self-governed nations do not fill their neighbor states with spies or set the course of intrigue to bring about some critical posture of affairs which will give them an opportunity to strike and make conquest. Such designs can be successfully worked only under cover and where no one has the right to ask questions.

Cunningly contrived plans of deception or aggression, carried, it may be, from generation to generation, can be worked out and kept from the light only within the privacy of courts or behind the carefully guarded confidences of a narrow and privileged class. They are happily impossible where public opinion commands and insists upon full information concerning all the nation's affairs.

PEACE THROUGH FREE PEOPLES

A steadfast concert for peace can never be maintained except by a partnership of democratic nations. No autocratic Government could be trusted to keep faith within it or observe its covenants. It must be a league of honor, a partnership of opinion. Intrigue would eat its vitals away, the plottings of inner circles who could plan what they would and render account to no one would be a corruption seated at its very heart. Only free peoples can hold their purpose and their honor steady to a common end and prefer the interests of mankind to any narrow interest of their own.

Does not every American feel that assurance has been added to our hope for the future peace of the world by the wonderful and heartening things that have been happening within the last few weeks in Russia?

Russia was known by those who know it best to have been always in fact democratic at heart, in all the vital habits of her thought, in all the intimate relationships of her people that spoke their natural instinct, their habitual attitude toward life.

Autocracy that crowned the summit of her political structure, long as it had stood and terrible as was the reality

41

of its power, was not in fact Russian in origin, in character or purpose; and now it has been shaken and the great, generous Russian people have been added, in all their native majesty and might, to the forces that are fighting for freedom in the world, for justice and for peace. Here is a fit partner for a league of honor.

One of the things that have served to convince us that the Prussian autocracy was not and could never be our friend is that from the very outset of the present war it has filled our unsuspecting communities and even our offices of Government with spies and set criminal intrigues everywhere afoot against our national unity of council, our peace within and without, our industries and our commerce.

Indeed, it is now evident that its spies were here even before the war began, and it is, unhappily, not a matter of conjecture, but a fact proved in our courts of justice, that the intrigues which have more than once come perilously near to disturbing the peace and dislocating the industries of the country have been carried on at the instigation, with the support, and even under the personal direction, of official agents of the Imperial German Government accredited to the Government of the United States.

Even in checking these things and trying to extirpate them we have sought to put the most generous interpretation possible upon them because we knew that their source lay, not in any hostile feeling or purpose of the

German people toward us (who were, no doubt, as ignorant of them as we ourselves were), but only in the selfish designs of a Government that did what it pleased and told its people nothing. But they have played their part in serving to convince us at last that that Government entertains no real friendship for us and means to act against our peace and security at its convenience. That it means to stir up enemies against us at our very doors the intercepted note to the German Minister at Mexico City is eloquent evidence.

A CHALLENGE OF HOSTILE PURPOSE

We are accepting this challenge of hostile purpose because we know that in such a Government, following such methods, we can never have a friend; and that in the presence of its organized power, always lying in wait to accomplish we know not what purpose, there can be no assured security for the democratic Governments of the world.

We are now about to accept the gage of battle with this natural foe to liberty, and shall, if necessary, spend the whole force of the nation to check and nullify its pretensions and its power. We are glad, now that we see the facts with no veil of false pretense about them, to fight thus for the ultimate peace of the world and for the liberation of its peoples, the German people included; for the rights of nations great and small and the privilege of men everywhere to choose their way of life and of obedience. The world must be made safe for democracy. Its peace must be planted upon the trusted foundations of political liberty.

We have no selfish ends to serve. We desire no conquest, no dominion. We seek no indemnities for ourselves, no material compensation for the sacrifices we shall freely make. We are but one of the champions of the rights of mankind. We shall be satisfied when those rights have been made as secure as the faith and the freedom of the nation can make them.

Just because we fight without rancor and without selfish objects, seeking nothing for ourselves but what we shall wish to share with all free peoples, we shall, I feel confident, conduct our operations as belligerents without passion and ourselves observe with proud punctilio the principles of right and of fair play we profess to be fighting for.

I have said nothing of the Governments allied with the Imperial Government of Germany because they have not made war upon us or challenged us to defend our right and our honor.

The Austro-Hungarian Government has indeed avowed its unqualified indorsement and acceptance of the reckless and lawless submarine warfare adopted now without disguise by the Imperial German Government, and it has therefore not been possible for this Government to receive Count Tarnowski, the ambassador recently accredited to this

Government by the Imperial and Royal Government of Austria-Hungary; but that Government has not actually engaged in warfare against citizens of the United States on the seas, and I take the liberty, for the present at least, of postponing a discussion of our relations with the authorities at Vienna.

OPPOSITION TO THE GERMAN GOVERNMENT
FRIENDSHIP TOWARD THE GERMAN PEOPLE

We enter this war only where we are clearly forced into it because there are no other means of defending our rights.

It will be all the easier for us to conduct ourselves as belligerents in a high spirit of right and fairness because we act without animus, not in enmity toward a people or with the desire to bring any injury or disadvantage upon them, but only in armed opposition to an irresponsible Government which has thrown aside all considerations of humanity and of right and is running amuck.

We are, let me say again, the sincere friends of the German people, and shall desire nothing so much as the early re-establishment of intimate relations of mutual advantage between us—however hard it may be for them, for the time being, to believe that this is spoken from our hearts. We have borne with their present Government through all these bitter months because of that friendship—

exercising a patience and forbearance which would otherwise have been impossible.

We shall, happily, still have an opportunity to prove that friendship in our daily attitude and actions toward the millions of men and women of German birth and native sympathy who live amongst us and share our life, and we shall be proud to prove it toward all who are, in fact, loyal to their neighbors and to the Government in the hour of test. They are, most of them, as true and loyal Americans as if they had never known any other fealty or allegiance. They will be prompt to stand with us in rebuking and restraining the few who may be of a different mind and purpose. If there should be disloyalty it will be dealt with with a firm hand of stern repression; but, if it lifts its head at all, it will lift it only here and there and without countenance except from a lawless and malignant few.

RIGHT MORE PRECIOUS THAN PEACE

It is a distressing and oppressive duty, gentlemen of the Congress, which I have performed in thus addressing you. There are, it may be, many months of fiery trial and sacrifice ahead of us. It is a fearful thing to lead this great, peaceful people into war, into the most terrible and disastrous of all wars, civilization itself seeming to be in the balance. But the right is more precious than peace, and we shall fight for the things which we have always carried nearest our hearts—for democracy, for the right of those who submit to authority to have a voice in their own governments, for the rights and liberties of small nations, for a universal dominion of right by such a concert of free peoples as shall bring peace and safety to all nations and make the world itself at last free.

To such a task we can dedicate our lives and our fortunes, everything that we are and everything that we have, with the pride of those who know that the day has come when America is privileged to spend her blood and her might for the principles that gave her birth and happiness and the peace which she has treasured. God helping her, she can do no other.

V.
A STATE OF WAR

The President's Proclamation of
April 6, 1917

Whereas the Congress of the United States in the exercise of the constitutional authority vested in them have resolved, by joint resolution of the Senate and House of Representatives bearing date this day "That the state of war between the United States and the Imperial German

Government which has been thrust upon the United States is hereby formally declared";

Whereas it is provided by Section 4067 of the Revised Statutes, as follows:

Whenever there is declared a war between the United States and any foreign nation or government, or any invasion or predatory incursion is perpetrated, attempted, or threatened against the territory of the United States, by any foreign nation or government, and the President makes public proclamation of the event, all natives, citizens, denizens, or subjects of a hostile nation or government, being males of the age of fourteen years and upwards, who shall be within the United States, and not actually naturalized, shall be liable to be apprehended, restrained, secured, and removed as alien enemies. The President is authorized, in any such event, by his proclamation thereof, or other public act, to direct the conduct to be observed, on the part of the United States, toward the aliens who become so liable; the manner and degree of the restraint to which they shall be subject, and in what cases, and upon what security their residence shall be permitted, and to provide for the removal of those who, not being permitted to reside within the United States, refuse or neglect to depart therefrom; and to establish any such regulations which are found necessary in the premises and for the public safety;

Whereas, by Sections 4068, 4069, and 4070 of the Revised Statutes, further provision is made relative to alien enemies;

Now, therefore, I, Woodrow Wilson, President of the United States of America, do hereby proclaim to all whom it may concern that a state of war exists between the United States and the Imperial German Government; and I do specially direct all officers, civil or military, of the United States that they exercise vigilance and zeal in the discharge of the duties incident to such a state of war; and I do, moreover, earnestly appeal to all American citizens that they, in loyal devotion to their country, dedicated from its foundation to the principles of liberty and justice, uphold the laws of the land, and give undivided and willing support to those measures which may be adopted by the constitutional authorities in prosecuting the war to a successful issue and in obtaining a secure and just peace;

And, acting under and by virtue of the authority vested in me by the Constitution of the United States and the said sections of the Revised Statutes, I do hereby further proclaim and direct that the conduct to be observed on the part of the United States toward all natives, citizens, denizens, or subjects of Germany, being males of the age of fourteen years and upwards, who shall be within the United States and not actually naturalized, who for the purpose of this proclamation and under such sections of the Revised Statutes are termed alien enemies, shall be as follows:

All alien enemies are enjoined to preserve the peace towards the United States and to refrain from crime against the public safety, and from violating the laws of the United States and of the States and Territories thereof, and to refrain from actual hostility or giving information, aid or comfort to the enemies of the United States, and to comply strictly with the regulations which are hereby or which may be from time to time promulgated by the President; and so long as they shall conduct themselves in accordance with law, they shall be undisturbed in the peaceful pursuit of their lives and occupations and be accorded the consideration due to all peaceful and law-abiding persons, except so far as restrictions may be necessary for their own protection and for the safety of the United States; and towards such alien enemies as conduct themselves in accordance with law, all citizens of the United States are enjoined to preserve the peace and to treat them with all such friendliness as may be compatible with loyalty and allegiance to the United States.

And all alien enemies who fail to conduct themselves as so enjoined, in addition to all other penalties prescribed by law, shall be liable to restraint, or to give security, or to remove and depart from the United States in the manner prescribed by Sections 4069 and 4070 of the Revised Statutes, and as prescribed in the regulations duly promulgated by the President;

And pursuant to the authority vested in me, I hereby declare and establish the following regulations, which I find necessary in the premises and for the public safety:

First. An alien enemy shall not have in his possession, at any time or place, any fire-arm, weapon or implement of war, or component part thereof, ammunition, maxim or other silencer, bomb or explosive or material used in the manufacture of explosives;

Second. An alien enemy shall not have in his possession at any time or place, or use or operate any aircraft or wireless apparatus, or any form of signalling device, or any form of cipher code, or any paper, document or book written or printed in cipher or in which there may be invisible writing;

Third. All property found in the possession of an alien enemy in violation of the foregoing regulations shall be subject to seizure by the United States;

Fourth. An alien enemy shall not approach or be found within one-half of a mile of any Federal or State fort, camp, arsenal, aircraft station, Government or naval vessel, navy yard, factory, or workshop for the manufacture of munitions of war or of any products for the use of the army or navy;

Fifth. An alien enemy shall not write, print, or publish any attack or threats against the Government or Congress of the United States, or either branch thereof, or against the measures or policy of the United States, or against the person or property of any person in the military, naval or civil service of the United States, or of the States or Territories, or of the District of Columbia, or of the municipal governments therein;

Sixth. An alien enemy shall not commit or abet any hostile acts against the United States, or give information, aid, or comfort to its enemies;

Seventh. An alien enemy shall not reside in or continue to reside in, to remain in, or enter any locality which the President may from time to time designate by Executive Order as a prohibited area in which residence by an alien enemy shall be found by him to constitute a danger to the public peace and safety of the United States, except by permit from the President and except under such limitations or restrictions as the President may prescribe;

Eighth. An alien enemy whom the President shall have reasonable cause to believe to be aiding or about to aid the enemy, or to be at large to the danger of the public peace or safety of the United States, or to have violated or to be about to violate any of these regulations, shall remove to any location designated by the President by Executive Order, and shall not remove therefrom without a permit, or shall depart from the United States if so required by the President;

Ninth. No alien enemy shall depart from the United States until he shall have received such permit as the President shall prescribe, or except under order of a court, judge, or justice, under Sections 4069 and 4070 of the Revised Statutes;

Tenth. No alien enemy shall land in or enter the United States, except under such restrictions and at such places as the President may prescribe;

Eleventh. If necessary to prevent violation of the regulations, all alien enemies will be obliged to register;

Twelfth. An alien enemy whom there may be reasonable cause to believe to be aiding or about to aid the enemy, or who may be at large to the danger of the public peace or safety, or who violates or attempts to violate, or of whom there is reasonable ground to believe that he is about to violate, any regulation duly promulgated by the President, or any criminal law of the United States, or of the States or Territories thereof, will be subject to summary arrest by the

53

United States Marshal, or his deputy, or such other officer as the President shall designate, and to confinement in such penitentiary, prison, jail, military camp, or other place of detention as may be directed by the President.

This proclamation and the regulations herein contained shall extend and apply to all land and water, continental or insular, in any way within the jurisdiction of the United States.

VI.
"SPEAK, ACT, AND SERVE TOGETHER"

Message to the American People
April 15, 1917

My Fellow-Countrymen:

The entrance of our own beloved country into the grim and terrible war for democracy and human rights which has shaken the world creates so many problems of national life and action which call for immediate consideration and settlement that I hope you will permit me to address to you a few words of earnest counsel and appeal with regard to them.

We are rapidly putting our navy upon an effective war footing and are about to create and equip a great army, but these are the simplest parts of the great task to which we have addressed ourselves. There is not a single selfish element, so far as I can see, in the cause we are fighting for. We are fighting for what we believe and wish to be the rights of mankind and for the future peace and security of the world. To do this great thing worthily and successfully we must devote ourselves to the service without regard to profit or material advantage and with an energy and intelligence that will rise to the level of the enterprise itself. We must realize to the full how great the task is and how many things, how many kinds and elements of capacity and service and self-sacrifice it involves.

WHAT WE MUST DO

These, then, are the things we must do, and do well, besides fighting—the things without which mere fighting would be fruitless:

We must supply abundant food for ourselves and for our armies and our seamen, not only, but also for a large part of the nations with whom we have now made common cause, in whose support and by whose sides we shall be fighting.

We must supply ships by the hundreds out of our shipyards to carry to the other side of the sea, submarines or no submarines, what will every day be needed there, and abundant materials out of our fields and our mines and our factories with which not only to clothe and equip our own forces on land and sea, but also to clothe and support our people, for whom the gallant fellows under arms can no longer work; to help clothe and equip the armies with which we are co-operating in Europe, and to keep the looms and manufactories there in raw material; coal to keep the fires going in ships at sea and in the furnaces of hundreds of factories across the sea; steel out of which to make arms and ammunition both here and there; rails for wornout railways back of the fighting fronts; locomotives and rolling-stock to take the place of those every day going to pieces; mules, horses, cattle for labor and for military service; everything with which the people of England and France and Italy and Russia have usually supplied themselves, but cannot now afford the men, the materials or the machinery to make.

GREATER EFFICIENCY

It is evident to every thinking man that our industries, on the farms, in the shipyards, in the mines, in the factories, must be made more prolific and more efficient than ever, and that they must be more economically managed and better adapted to the particular requirements of our task than they have been; and what I want to say is that the men and the women who devote their thought and their energy to these things will be serving the country and conducting the fight for peace and freedom just as truly and just as effectively as the men on the battle-field or in the trenches. The industrial forces of the country, men and women alike, will be a great national, a great international, service army— a notable and honored host engaged in the service of the nation and the world, the efficient friends and saviors of free men everywhere. Thousands, nay, hundreds of thousands, of men otherwise liable to military service will of right and of necessity be excused from that service and assigned to the fundamental sustaining work of the fields and factories and mines, and they will be as much part of the great patriotic forces of the nation as the men under fire.

THE RESPONSIBILITY OF THE FARMERS

I take the liberty, therefore, of addressing this word to the farmers of the country and to all who work on the farms: The supreme need of our own nation and of the nations with which we are co-operating is an abundance of supplies, and especially of foodstuffs. The importance of an adequate food-supply, especially for the present year, is superlative. Without abundant food, alike for the armies and the peoples now at war, the whole great enterprise upon which we have embarked will break down and fail. The world's food reserves are low. Not only during the present emergency, but for some time after peace shall have come, both our own people and a large proportion of the people of Europe must rely upon the harvests in America.

Upon the farmers of this country, therefore, in large measure rests the fate of the war and the fate of the nations. May the nation not count upon them to omit no step that will increase the production of their land or that will bring about the most effectual co-operation in the sale and distribution of their products? The time is short. It is of the most imperative importance that everything possible be done, and done immediately, to make sure of large harvests. I call upon young men and old alike and upon the able-bodied boys of the land to accept and act upon this duty—to turn in hosts to the farms and make certain that no pains and no labor is lacking in this great matter.

I particularly appeal to the farmers of the South to plant abundant foodstuffs, as well as cotton. They can show their patriotism in no better or more convincing way than by resisting the great temptation of the present price of cotton and helping, helping upon a great scale, to feed the nation and the peoples everywhere who are fighting for their liberties and for our own. The variety of their crops will be the visible measure of their comprehension of their national duty.

The Government of the United States and the Governments of the several States stand ready to co-operate. They will do everything possible to assist farmers in securing an adequate supply of seed, an adequate force of laborers when they are most needed, at harvest-time, and the means of expediting shipments of fertilizers and farm machinery, as well as of the crops themselves when harvested. The course of trade shall be as unhampered as it is possible to make it, and there shall be no unwarranted manipulation of the nation's food-supply by those who handle it on its way to the consumer. This is our opportunity to demonstrate the efficiency of a great democracy, and we shall not fall short of it!

THE DUTY OF MIDDLEMEN

This let me say to the middlemen of every sort, whether they are handling our foodstuffs or the raw materials of manufacture or the products of our mills and factories: The eyes of the country will be especially upon you. This is your opportunity for signal service, efficient and disinterested. The country expects you, as it expects all others, to forego unusual profits, to organize and expedite shipments of supplies of every kind, but especially of food, with an eye to the service you are rendering and in the spirit of those who enlist in the ranks, for their people, not for themselves. I shall confidently expect you to deserve and win the confidence of people of every sort and station.

THE MEN OF THE RAILWAYS

To the men who run the railways of the country, whether they be managers or operative employees, let me say that the railways are the arteries of the nation's life and that upon them rests the immense responsibility of seeing to it that those arteries suffer no obstruction of any kind, no inefficiency or slackened power. To the merchant let me suggest the motto, "Small profits and quick service," and to the shipbuilder the thought that the life of the war depends upon him. The food and the war supplies must be carried across the seas, no matter how many ships are sent to the bottom. The places of those that go down must be supplied, and supplied at once. To the miner let me say that he stands where the farmer does: the work of the world waits on him. If he slackens or fails, armies and statesmen are helpless. He also is enlisted in the great Service Army. The manufacturer does not need to be told, I hope, that the nation looks to him to speed and perfect every process; and I want only to remind his employees that their service is absolutely indispensable and is counted on by every man who loves the country and its liberties.

Let me suggest also that every one who creates or cultivates a garden helps, and helps greatly, to solve the problem of the feeding of the nations; and that every housewife who practises strict economy puts herself in the ranks of those who serve the nation. This is the time for America to correct her unpardonable fault of wastefulness and extravagance. Let every man and every woman assume the duty of careful, provident use and expenditure as a public duty, as a dictate of patriotism which no one can now expect ever to be excused or forgiven for ignoring.

THE SUPREME TEST

In the hope that this statement of the needs of the nation and of the world in this hour of supreme crisis may stimulate those to whom it comes and remind all who need reminder of the solemn duties of a time such as the world has never seen before, I beg that all editors and publishers everywhere will give as prominent publication and as wide circulation as possible to this appeal. I venture to suggest also to all advertising agencies that they would perhaps render a very substantial and timely service to the country if they would give it widespread repetition. And I hope that clergymen will not think the theme of it an unworthy or inappropriate subject of comment and homily from their pulpits.

The supreme test of the nation has come. We must all speak, act, and serve together!

CONTENTS